NATURE SPY

NATURE SPY

written by SHELLEY ROTNER and KEN KREISLER
photographs by SHELLEY ROTNER

Atheneum Books for Young Readers

Atheneum Books for Young Readers
An imprint of Simon & Schuster Children's Publishing Division
1230 Avenue of the Americas
New York, New York 10020

The text of this book is set in 18 pt. Meridien.
Printed in Hong Kong
First Edition
10   9   8   7   6   5   4   3

Library of Congress Cataloging-in-Publication Data
Rotner, Shelley. Nature spy / written by Shelley Rotner and Ken Kreisler :
photographs by Shelley Rotner. — 1st ed.   p.   cm. Summary: A child
takes a close-up look at such aspects of nature as an acorn, the golden eye of
a frog, and an empty hornet's nest. ISBN 0-02-777885-1   1. Nature—Juvenile
literature. [I. Nature.] I. Kreisler, Ken. II. Title.
QH48.R655   1992   508—dc20   91-38430

For Emily, my little nature spy
—S. R.

For Linda, dream a little dream with me
—K. K.

I like to go outside—to look around and discover things.

To take a really close look, even closer

and closer.

My mother says I'm a curious kid. She calls me a nature spy.

Sometimes I look so closely, I can see the lines on a shiny green leaf,

or one small acorn on a branch,

or seeds in a pod.

I notice the feathers of a bird,

or the golden eye of a frog.

When you look closely, things look so different—
like the bark of a tree or an empty hornet's nest,

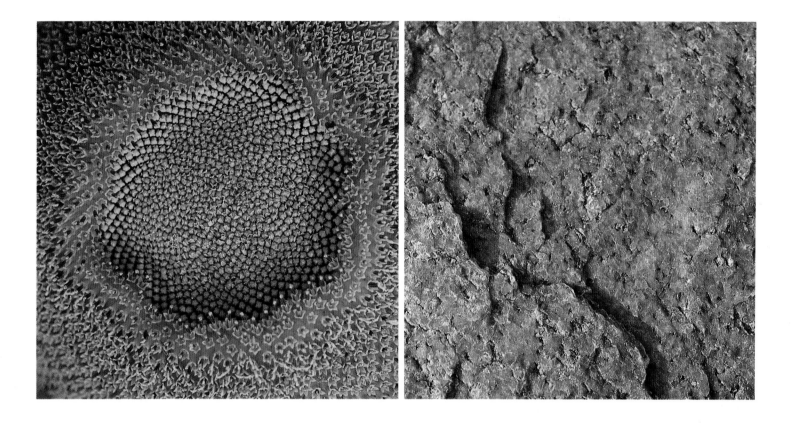

the seeds of a sunflower, or even a rock.

Sometimes there's a pattern, like ice on a frozen pond,

or a spider's web, or a butterfly's wing.

Everything has its own shape, color,

and size.

Look closely at a turtle's shell,

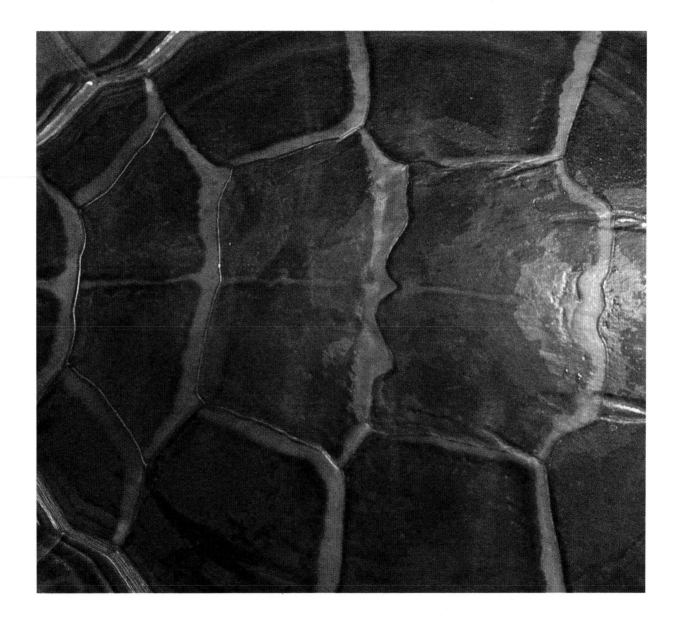

or a dog's fur,

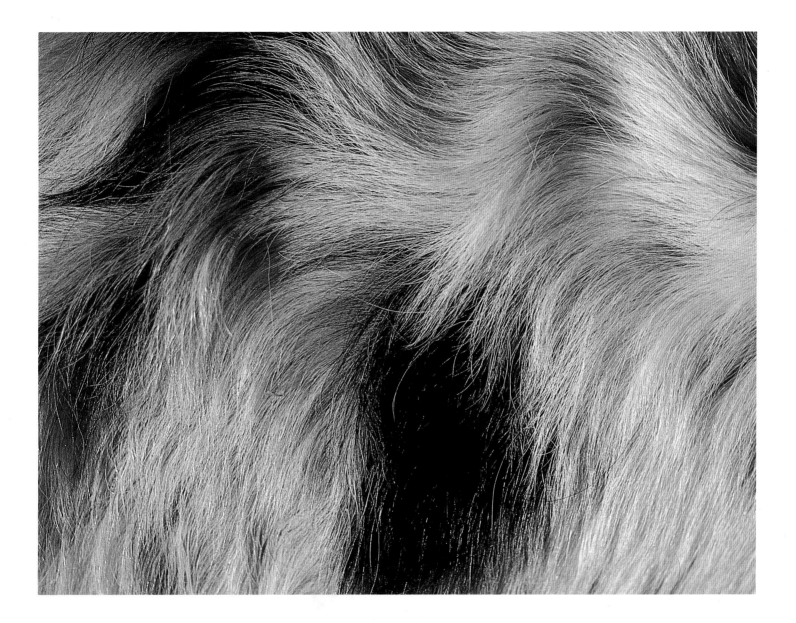

or even raspberries,

or kernels of corn.

No matter where you look, up, down

or all around,

there's always something to see
when you're a nature spy!